# Beyond the Ridge

PAUL GOBLE

*What is life?*
*It is the flash of a firefly in the night.*
*It is the breath of a buffalo in the wintertime*
*It is the little shadow that runs across the*
*grass and loses itself in the sunset.*

*Man's life is brief,*
*and being so it is useless to have the fear of death,*
*for death must come sooner or later to everybody.*
*Man and all living things are born,*
*pass on and are gone,*
*while the mountains and the rivers remain*
*always the same—*
*these alone of all visible things stay unchanged.*

*Death comes,*
*and always comes out of season.*
*It is the command of the Great Spirit.*
*All nations and people must obey.*

# Beyond the Ridge

Story and illustrations by PAUL GOBLE

ALADDIN BOOKS
Macmillan Publishing Company   *New York*
Maxwell Macmillan Canada   *Toronto*
Maxwell Macmillan International   *New York   Oxford   Singapore   Sydney*

*for Richard*

First Aladdin Books edition 1993

Aladdin Books                          Maxwell Macmillan Canada, Inc.
Macmillan Publishing Company           1200 Eglinton Avenue East
866 Third Avenue                       Suite 200
New York, NY 10022                     Don Mills, Ontario M3C 3N1

Macmillan Publishing Company is part of the Maxwell Communication Group of
Companies.
Printed in the United States of America
10  9  8  7  6  5  4  3  2
A hardcover edition of *Beyond the Ridge* is available from Bradbury Press, an affiliate of
Macmillan, Inc.

Library of Congress Cataloging-in-Publication Data
Goble, Paul.
    Beyond the ridge / story and illustrations by Paul Goble—1st Aladdin Books ed.
      p.    cm.
    Includes bibliographical references.
    Summary: At her death an elderly Plains Indian woman experiences the afterlife
believed in by her people, while the surviving family members prepare her body
according to their custom.
    ISBN 0-689-71731-8
    1. Indians of North America—Great Plains—Juvenile fiction. [1. Indians of North
America—Great Plains—Fiction.]   I. Title.
[PZ7.G5384Be   1993]
[E]—dc20   92-39786

SOURCES: The passages printed in italic were spoken by Indian people, and come from the following books:
"What is life?" from *Canadian Portraits*, Ethel Brant Monture, Irwin and Company Ltd., Toronto, 1960. "Man's
life is brief" from *The Omaha Tribe*, Alice Fletcher and Francis LaFlesche, 27th Annual Report of the Bureau of
American Ethnology, Washington, D.C., 1911. "Death comes" from *Four Corners of the Sky*, Theodore Clymer,
Little, Brown and Company, Boston, 1975. "This land is beautiful" from *Songs of the Teton Sioux*, Harry W. Paige,
Westernlore Press, Los Angeles, 1970. "Anything that has a birth" and "No man knows" from *Lakota Belief and
Ritual*, James R. Walker, edited by Raymond J. DeMaille and Elaine A. Jahner, University of Nebraska Press,
Lincoln, 1980; edited by Paul Goble. "Death?" from *Touch the Earth*, T. C. McLuhan, Abacus, London, 1973.
"*Wakan Tanka*" from *Teton Sioux Music*, Frances Densmore, Bureau of American Ethnology, Washington, D.C.,
1918.

REFERENCES: Grinnell, George Bird, *The Cheyenne Indians*, Yale University Press, New Haven, 1923. Hassrick,
Royal B., *The Sioux*, University of Oklahoma Press, Norman, 1964. Marriott, Alice and Carol K. Rachlin, *American
Indian Mythology*, Thomas Y. Crowell Company, New York, 1968.

In this book I have embroidered upon a few of the thoughts which Plains Indian people express. Dying, they say, is like climbing up a long and difficult slope towards a high pine-covered ridge on the Great Plains. From the top we shall see, *beyond the ridge*, the Spirit World, the Land of Many Tipis, the place from which we came, and the place to which we shall return. It will be like this world, they say, except that we shall perceive it as even more beautiful, and with a greater abundance of birds and animals. We shall live there without fatigue or sorrow or illness.

The clothes and blankets illustrated date from the last quarter of the nineteenth century, the period when trade cloth had largely taken the place of skins. Navajo blankets were popular among the people who lived on the Great Plains.

The old woman carries sage leaves; these are much used in ceremonies because they are "pleasing to the spirits." Crows appear in several pictures, for it is said that the Crow is often a messenger of the spirits, although help from the spirits comes in many other forms.

Faces are drawn without any expression or features. (This follows the convention of traditional Indian hide and ledger-book painting, and even children's dolls.) I once asked a Lakota lady, who makes dolls dressed in every minute detail, why she left the faces without features. Her reply was that children give the dolls their own personality, and do not have it dictated to them by the maker.

A single outline technique is used for the drawing. This is worked out in pencil and then is drawn in ink, and the pencil lines are erased. The color is watercolor, both opaque and transparent, and applied almost up to the pen outline; this has the effect of leaving thin "white lines" which give brightness and clarity to the painting.

This land is beautiful.
O Sun,
now for the last time,
come greet me again.

An old woman lay on her bed. She had lain there for many days. She could not get up. She was dying. The medicine men had done all they could. Her husband and her daughter and grandchildren were beside her.

The old woman heard a voice saying, "Get up! They want you over there. Your mother is calling you." She did not understand; her mother had died many years before. "Your mother is calling you," the voice said again.

The old woman got up, and as she left the tipi, she turned and saw herself lying under her blanket, with all her family around her. They looked sad and worried. "My mother is calling me. I must go to her," she told them, and yet she did not think that they heard. Her dogs knew that they could not go with her.

The voice seemed to lead her away from the camp, towards a high pine-covered ridge. As she started to climb she realized that she was wearing her favorite dress and moccasins. She did not remember putting them on. She knew that she had to climb up to the ridge, but it was so faraway—and so high. She did not think she could ever reach the top.

4

Her tipi was faraway behind her, but she could plainly
hear her husband speaking. She heard him say, "I do
not think she is breathing any longer." Her grandchildren
were crying. She wanted to go back and tell them not
to be sad, because now she was up again and feeling
better. The words would not come, and her feet led
her slowly up towards some great boulders and pine
trees near the top.

"Listen! Your mother calls you," the voice said.
She listened. She could not hear her mother calling.
She climbed on.

When at last she approached the ridge, she could glimpse a view between the pine trees. And then, over the tops of the weathered boulders, she saw a country stretching blue and green into the distance.

It was the most wonderful view that she had ever seen. Cooling breezes moved up the slopes from that beautiful country on the other side. Everywhere she looked there were butterflies and birds. Everywhere there were herds of buffalo and antelope.

The ground was bright with flowers and sloped gently
down towards a river and a circle of tipis.

She could still hear her grandchildren crying. She wanted to go back. She had to tell them there was no need to cry. "They want you over there," she again heard the voice. "Your mother is calling you."

And then she could hear! Ah, the voice she knew so well! She looked down towards the circle of tipis, and there was her mother walking with arms outstretched. She was smiling, and looked young and happy. And behind her mother were her father and grandparents, and all the people she had known who had died long ago.

She felt strong again. The way down from the top was so easy and beautiful. She even wanted to run. There was no other path to take.

Anything that has a birth, must also have a death.
The spirit is not born with a person,
but is given at the time of birth.
Therefore, because the spirit has no birth,
it will never die.

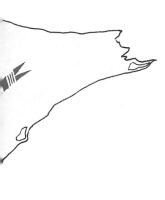

Her husband and her daughter and grandchildren knew that her shadow was travelling towards the Land of Many Tipis. She was dead. Now it was only her body which lay on the bed. An awful feeling of loneliness and emptiness took hold of everyone who had gathered in the tipi. But there were things to do: the women washed her, and they put on her blue cloth dress which had elk teeth sewn all over it. They combed and braided her hair and painted her face with red paint. They placed beside her all the things which she had been used to and had enjoyed when she was alive: her awl and knife, her elkhorn hide scraper, her paints and quill-embroidery bag. The spirits of those things would pass with her shadow into the Spirit World.

They wrapped her in a buffalo robe which she had once painted. They tied it tightly. They would never see her face again; nobody could take her place.

They took her away from the camp along the creek and put her on a platform among the branches of an old cottonwood tree. The earth would soon take back her body, and her spirit would be free in the winds and clouds.

Her family stayed under the tree. They brought food for her journey along the Pathway of the Souls. They did not want her to leave them. They felt they would always cry. Even the crows were mourning.

Death seems like the end, but it is not. The body goes back to the earth, but the spirit lives forever. We are not left alone; the dead, and the living, and those who will one day be born are part of a great circle. We are all together within this circle. It is so! Praise the Creator, the Great Spirit!

19

The pathway of this life leads into the pathway of the next life. Those who have gone *beyond the ridge* travel south along the Milky Way, the Spirit Trail, the Ghost Road. We can see it hanging in the night sky, the trail illuminated by the myriad campfires of the spirits moving towards the Spirit World. We shall reach a fork in the trail where there sits an old woman called *Hinhan Kara*, Owl Maker. Those who have led good lives pass her to the right, towards *Wanagiyata*, the Land of Many Tipis. Those who have led bad lives she pushes to the left along a short path where the spirits fall off, back to earth, to wander for a time as ghosts.

No man knows where the Spirit World is.
The ancient people said that it is beyond the pines.
The pine trees are at the edge of the world,
and beyond them is the path of the winds.
The Spirit Way begins there at the edge of the world
among the stars, and the winds will tell the spirits of
people where to find it.

Death?
There is no death;
only a change of worlds.

*WAKAN TANKA*, Great Spirit, we call upon you:
Have pity on us.
Give us the strength to be right and honest
in all we do.
Give us the strength to live a long life.

When a person goes to a hilltop to pray,
offerings are left for the spirits:
cloth, string of tobacco, eagle feather,
pipe, buffalo skull, etc.